Reckless Wedding

Reckless Wedding

MARIA FLOOK

HOUGHTON MIFFLIN COMPANY BOSTON

1982

Library of Congress Cataloging in Publication Data
Flook, Maria.   Reckless wedding.
(The Houghton Mifflin new poetry series)
I. Title.   II. Series.
PS3556.L583R4   1982   811'.54   82-9312
ISBN 0-395-32507-2   AACR2
ISBN 0-395-32508-0 (pbk.)

Printed in the United States of America

V 10 9 8 7 6 5 4 3 2 1

Acknowledgments

Some of these poems have previously appeared in the following publications, to whose editors grateful acknowledgment is made: *Agni Review, Aldebaran, American Poetry Review, Antioch Review, Iowa Review, Pavement,* and *Shankpainter.* "The Late-Shift Comptroller" and "Strangers: Many Perfect Examples" first appeared in *Poetry.*

"Missing from Home" is dedicated to Anne Sullivan; "Strangers: Many Perfect Examples" is dedicated to Jayne Anne Phillips; "Tuesday" is for John Skoyles. I am grateful to The Fine Arts Work Center in Provincetown, to the poet Robert McRoberts, and to my parents for their support.

for Kate

Contents

One

The Childlike Lives of the
Sweep Second Hand and the Single Mother

When I miss someone small
I can't admit it. I don't tell
my daughter that we sleepwalk together
and go to opposite corners of the house.
Who are we looking for?
There is a room to be filled.
We seem restless to begin
a more accurate fumbling
through the dark.

Sometimes I want to press my cheek
against the spine of a fat woman.
It will be a kind of love
but it will have its back to me.
You are so tiny
and must always face me.
I keep for you this space
comfortable as the armchair
made of snow, but warm
like a mare's placenta.

Once you were vanishing, curled up
into the black periwinkle, little magnet
gripping the ore in a stone, and sinking.
Now you grow, adding serious moments
like ounces to a scale.
As women we hold our clocks.
We measure how sad we are
by how much of the face falls into the hands.

The Late-Shift Comptroller

The dog has snapped its leash again.
A girl gets into a taxi
and into another taxi, and another.
The dark is sheer
and efficient as a blueprint
for truly modern tenements of night,
as the architects of suicide
draw up some final touches.

A woman with a black eye is going to a party.

The man who left his wife
yesterday,
is having second thoughts about tonight.
He imagines his wife upon the ruffled pillow
of orgasm, gripped by her single fantasy
like a tight glove.
How can he abandon her like this,
to such a willing dream?
He raises his arm at the yellow curb
but the taxis are filled with girls.
Is it the same girl,
and what is her destination?

A woman with a black eye is taking off her shoes.

He sits on the steps of a church,
the man
with the big decisions. The church doors
have no handles, there is no way in or out.
Angels in their dark invisible bodies are caught
laughing. The stoplight says yes,

no, yes. Now he desires his wife, now his blood
divides, now his sex prays —
right about then
there goes the girl in the taxi.
How her hair stays in place, how big are her eyes.

Under a blue net, spidery stars
are trapped like flies.
The moon is dissolving, cherry of morphine,
on someone's tongue. Why is the rape victim
still singing? And, the choir of crash-ups
so perfect —
from a thousand secret offices,
with the fat pencil
of twisted hearts,
madness decorates the charts.
Here the streets are fluorescent
as the trails of rats.
Here mysteries have numbers.
Like this, with half a world behind
desire, it goes on:
Night plans more nights.

It Can't Be from Love

I admire his attempt to come back,
like the boy who shot all the rats
at the dump, and afterwards feels empty.
Next Sunday, there will be more rats
and he'll get them too. As in the tailpipes
of junked cars they praise themselves,
multiplying so fast, it can't be from love.
He might think death begins this way, bald
and gnawing.

I read a letter he wrote to a woman
before he became like this.
His face appeared in a photograph
squinting, as if blinded by chrome.
I wish he had written the letter to me,
back when he believed what he said.
As we believed he aimed at nothing
but love, having explained it
realistically, using action verbs
and the disheartened pronoun, *her*.
Describing wrecks on the highway and girls
in winter as pretty targets for snowballs,
he had a knack for exposing things.
What we hoped were lies, turned out true.

I know what it's like to sit behind
a wheel that does not turn, and wait.
Abandoned things sometimes become memorable,
suddenly cherished, and I'm hopeful.
Desire makes an engine's loud noise,
but to him it is the roar of inertia
like rodents eating through a steel womb.

If he gave everything over to love,
and it left without saying why, or *Sorry*,
let me. I'll take all the blame, so he won't
blame love. But some things must want to be
left alone, like hearts
that just grow larger with neglect.

For a Father

Inside his serious desk,
the black cardboard silhouette
of a fourth grader maintains
its crisp profile.
One blue valentine
from a teenager on probation
is turning violet.

If we take a colored slide
and hold it up,
the little girls inside
show us how far we have gone.
The lamp behind, cool white —
some call this cruelty.

Remember the grassy hill
where a father
made the movies.
Two daughters
somersaulted single file
until they rolled out of view.

And if he called them back
they did not listen,
it was better to keep tumbling.
Pink seersucker deepened
a blood-like green.
Into the dark
they fell.

Poem for Prevention

Like a child in a well
dream Jack, dream Jill.
Beware these clumsy partners,
depend on no one.

The lamb strangles in petticoats.
Heidi flat on her back in edelweiss,
her sighs won't echo three times.
Children lose messages unless hypnotized.

Tucking a daughter to sleep
I fold the collar of my night.
When she falls from her bed
it is death practicing.

Hard surfaces will hold
until the sun peels off
the scar. How tired you are
of the moon,
tilting its same bruise.

A depth expands,
milk pupil
blue mouth
I no longer feed.

You began in me
that night below the cistern.
Love never rinses through,
it dries and makes
the lace old mothers wear.

Snow Statement

When weather makes someone
turn back, more than traffic
is delayed by this cold.
Behind frozen windshields,
people never meet
one another's promises.
It's dangerous to come and go;
they say the arc of a bridge
freezes first, and there
we lose control.
Better to stay alone and wait
where a child's red mitten
falls like a heart
half-buried in snow.

The wind builds its monument
and sings one colorless hymn.
What is left unprotected
becomes winter, black-fingered,
forcing in.
No use listening for footsteps,
snow soundproofs all things:
It's hard to recall
the hurt in someone's voice,
the way numb figures, stumbling,
can't feel bones break.

A skater moves greedily
across a lake, as if following
the profile on a coin.
Others circling the edge
have nothing to go on.

It falls, a whole year's blame
like an open letter,
a list of one name.
Yet, there is a footprint
love makes
when it walks out of the body.
An imprint so deep
snow can't fill it,
like the darkness in a room
behind white curtains.

The Crippled Heart

My daughter next to me
waits for the parade to press through.
She will meet the ankles of clowns
in silky harlequin and learn secrets.
She will see dark between the legs
of a majorette and think things
I can no longer think of.

We see a little boy in a wheelchair
riding a float. A large paper heart
circles his seat, made of paste
and shoe boxes, painted the milk-pink
of ballet slippers.
My daughter envies him, he has a radio
in his lap. She is jealous and angry
and she thinks the boy is lucky.
Running after him, she disappears.
She will like music and be attracted
to fancy vehicles, it's natural,
I know.

But I see something terrible,
something in the heart.
Empty boxes filling with shoes,
children carried helplessly forward
in a march.
My daughter strolls alongside
the boy, she almost touches him.
I can hear his radio,
a noise like suction.

I know that in other towns
they are building floats,
spelling words with paper blossoms.
I want it to be raining,
I want the heart to swell and collapse.
And the boy, who is dialing his radio
with a single, powerful hand —
I want him to slide from his platform
and roll down a steep street
out of my daughter's mind.

Poison Cloud

When Pam Snyder bleached her hair,
high, frozen cheeks burning —
the neighborhood changed.
I was always lonely, nothing
surprised me. Even when the sky
turned yellow and the smog
from Chester went out of control,
it was nothing
but an awful light.
The laundry was ruined again,
mothers wept
pulling the lines.
Everyone was worried about
the cold war and then brain tumors.

We went down to the warehouse
where boys had smashed
the vending machines
for nickels and quarters.
Circled by heavy blocks of chrome,
her white head
sliced open by mirrors
created a shattered light.
It was the first time
I felt lost, as she danced
in front of 30¢ cigarettes
looking like all of the Shirelles.

"If there's a bomb
we'll hide right here
until half the world is gone."
She promised me this. But she wouldn't

let her roots grow out, she had a toothbrush
and a bottle of peroxide.
Dividing her hair with her hands
she rubbed it hard
like money.

Nothing happened.
My hair grew long and black
and I fell in
with someone new.
I was stolen away, my mother said,
just in time.
Sometimes my palms get hot
as if I am holding fire
or a beautiful face
is breaking into sharp pieces.

I saw her in Ronnie's Corvette
a wound-up light in her head.
Like summer blindness, no one
could reach her or touch her fast enough.
Even the boy, who might have been happy,
was forced to look straight ahead
sunk low, and driving into it.

Talking Back

He turns up everywhere
alone. A road is narrow
and his shadow needs room.
Or his feet have reasons to leave
their single tracks,
as if to repeat the same syllables
clearly.
As a baby, he learned to walk.
It was like trying to spell a word,
a name to get up and fall down with.

It's hard to talk about love
and walk away.
Dogs follow men who leave home
as if a silent whistle was sounded,
and hunger wants to curl up and sleep
in someone's lap.
The neighbors, who turn on and off
their lights, are curious to see
how far he must get lost in love
to find a place.

Maybe when he's named each mongrel
without knowing their faces.
Or further on, if something aches behind
the knees. As in sex, a sensation
of having traveled a long way, perhaps
in the wrong direction.
Better for the legs to ache
than hearts.
Even a hundred heartbeats
cannot match this mystery, or tell

the truth like this:
The sound of his heels on an empty
sidewalk, when the pavement speaks
for him, some hard interpretation.
It's a way a man can move from love
and to love, talk back.

Imaginary Photograph of
Myself Holding a Pumpkin

The garden was not mine,
yet I opened the picket gate
as if I had planted everything.
Barefoot I walked over thin lace
of manure and through
the trellis of peas, between rows
of white lettuce as if everything
were mine. I skirted the red wasps
believing they too were forming
a flower, rootless, beside me.
I followed one long, prickly vine
until the end, and there I found it,
beneath dark leaves, tight as a handgrenade.

My neighbors watched me from a kitchen window
turning their backs to the glass
when I came out, my hands black with peat,
but empty. Soon they were no longer surprised,
they began to smile at me and wave.
For I had no basket, no paper sack heavy
with peppers. My shift was plain
without a secret apron of beans.

The pumpkin grew more round,
took color, the ironic hue of rust, like new steel.
When leaves began to wither in October,
with frost in my nostrils
and over the backyards, I walked
the delicate crust, not soil or memory.
Past the trellis of spiders, bodies
too cold to move, fat with a hundred days of winter
that would hatch from their stomachs.

I reached, lifting the pumpkin like an infant
from its black bedding.
Something went fleeing, a swarm that hovered
like one bewildered spirit.

My neighbors met me on the grass,
opening their cameras.
Feeling the cold, hard shell,
I stood perfectly still
and held it against my waist.

A New Career

A carpenter abandons his tools,
his wife. Too handsome for manual labor
he gets a job as "The Arrow Collar Man."

Road maps fanning open blow loose and fade.
The hot glove compartment driven elsewhere
waits to explode.
Romance is like blueprinting confused,
frail as tissue paper.
Bright as the secret of origami,
and quick as a firecracker.
It's a trick: wave good-bye to the bride
and spill the fist of rice, your hope
bleaches its trail.

Let's face it, she was ditched.
It's as simple as that, and during a war.
Her breath came hot and important
as riveting. News is: The Arrow Collar Man
has joined up. Stationed in Times Square
he recruits fifty WACs a day.

A beautiful veil, unbearable heat.
A *big* ceremony.
Over Japan a white hyacinth rises
building a poison roof.
It becomes the terrible corsage
at another wedding, a new career.

Ants in a White Peony

More than I counted on,
one by one
ants empty from the pale folds.
A single peony
pulled from its bush, a child
licking her lips offers me this.
Petals swell open like a mouth
filling with snow, or like a birth
with the small streak of red.
But birth is easier than this.

I fear abandonment in everything.
I've learned its sudden touch:
a small hand waving good-bye
underwater, or a secret landmark
that disappears overnight —
now the road doubles back
over black sand.
Ants walk to the white edges
of a flower, a map
we are wrong to follow.

It was necessary to leave
our summer homes, where childhood
seemed perennial.
Mothers no longer generous,
shaking their aprons of sugar,
do not call us back.
The peony
fully bloomed, loosens in its jar.
The child goes hunting for the queen,
snapping stems. With science she ignores
her new bouquet.

The Icehouse Mystery

How did the prisoner escape?
From a small room
he disappeared,
but why would he leave her?
The walls are smooth
like a secret sandblasted
again and again.

She wonders:
Is strength warm or cold?
She begins to get cold,
but nurses say she is better,
she is over the hump.
Soon she will be released.
These are the lies marching
in quiet white hosiery.

In Storm Lake, where he was born,
his grandfather ran the icehouse.
She dreams about it. There was fire,
it began with gloves on a lantern.
An ancestor, displaying a trait,
was falling in love
against his will.

The lunatic rehearses her kiss.
If you feed a blaze with snow
it gurgles like a mouth.
In the hospital
the lovesick melt away.

For sleep there are iron tongs,
like the pair that dragged cold blocks
into the sun. Or like the forceps
that delivered him violently.
He hated her arms
which could not hold him still.

When he was gone
she remembered the remote light
in his palms, how it offered no warmth
and made her world black.

Crime Wave

The inefficiency of petty thieves
creates humor in newspaper headlines,
when people are caught
holding on to what seems worthless.
I tried to walk away with love,
to possess it like something small
and taken at random.
Only a few others, standing close,
seemed to notice.

No one apprehended in love
can deny his part in it.
They say premeditation begins
with lust, when dreams progress secretly
as engineering. Innocence is a wordlessness
earned by the dead.
Mostly, it's impulse,
like peeling the varnish from public property
or writing a name on some bridge
above a freeway.
Desire spills its paint at night,
or in broad daylight goes out
a revolving door
underneath a woman's clothing.

After this, it's hard to return.
As when you enter a department store
and the cashier keeps an eye on you.
I wanted to give everything back, and I took
a taxi but could not describe the place.
Between dark buildings,
I saw people leave their friends

and mark the spot with colored chalk.
More privately, even hearts become defaced.
It happened when I recognized the initials
of someone I once knew,
and I just felt more alone.
Behind me, another waits
and another to steal his place,
to step from one shadow to the next.

Two

In Love

In love, keep yourself half dead.
Wear white or wear black.
Rise up like smoke, or wait
as a stone beneath it.
Think of fog, hard rain, deep snow.
Remember the long walk through sand.
Never travel back
with the heart, or trust it
much with maps and landmarks.
Take an alternate street
and chase away every little dog.
Let go of sentiment's heavy chain.
Forget hunger, let it stray behind
tall buildings. Fill its stomach with ice.
Don't stand in the dark hoping
for small things to happen.
If a shade snaps open, or a light
goes on, keep walking. Look down,
underneath your own shadow.
Recite the recipe for glass, make prayers
with sand. Cut your lips with a beautiful
name. Then go to the red and blue lounges;
memorize legs and faces
as they appear flickering
under musical lights.
Drink until the heart and mind of it
are swallowed.
Sleep with one foot on the floor,
let dreams walk away
and never come back.
Turn like a wheel with night

and break apart, become two clear pieces.
Rain will surprise you with emergency bells.
The sun, in its coat of white light,
will attend you.
Another day holds a mirror to your lips.

Freeze

In winter, romance breaks
like a cold pipe.
Don't be alarmed
when plumbers tear up the floor
to get to the problem,
or if a face drops out of reach
suddenly, with the absurdity
of a record temperature.
On the window, ice has formed
a shape so erotic, you can't mourn
but only shiver.

A woman left in a bright red sweater,
another arrived in a darker fashion.
In love, as in funeral processions,
grief should be worn, or shame
knits uncomfortable stitches over the body.
A furnace is inspected by authorities;
the answer appears to be ashes.
The cold must be kept out
like a figure standing on the corner
for hours
where snow mends sorrow into white clothing.

Radio Request

We are not speaking, something terrible
happened. It was the weekend when they
took the fishing boats out of the water
and hauled them away on flatbed trailers.
He went back to the city
but I stayed.
The sea is the same, glad to get
the weight off its back.
Fish have returned
to their practice of hiding
in light.

I wanted to send the pink crab shell;
it broke in half, its blood was sand.
I mailed instead the blue and white stones
that must be placed in a bowl of water
and studied like eyeballs.
He didn't see the point in it,
and the stones turned grey. There is no way
to reach him now. Even the ferry has quit;
it has swallowed the happy families
and it will be fat all winter.

I call the radio station;
my voice pricked by static
has become familiar to strangers.
From so far away,
I am expected to sound weak.
It pleases me to know that the same music
arrives in a thousand rooms.
I don't care what people think

when a song implies that something terrible
has happened.
I want him to recognize the tune
we whistled all summer, in pool rooms
on the pier, at the edge of love and
black water.
I want him to remember the last hard wave
that could not follow through, and turned back.
Why is it that something drowned
never keeps quiet?

It is difficult to humiliate desire;
that in itself is important to note,
if it is late at night
and someone is saying, "This is for that girl
on the island, God bless her."
The sea is the same. I am the same. Fish swim
to the false surface of the searchlight.

Strangers: Many Perfect Examples

I admit I have cheated, I held out
my hands and pretended to have nothing.
You stepped up to me
out of a dark building. You offered
the bread and the jewels; you wrote
your signature across blank lines.
You poured the wine,
my glass forgot the taste of emptiness,
all memory splashed red.
You put your lips upon my lips!
In public, our transactions appeared
honest. We walked together in parks
where a child handed me the last violet.
At the races, I bet on the horse named
Fascination, and it won.
Hallways filled with women who, at last,
seemed to know me.
Mirrors flattered me, the wind caressed
me with freshness. An ordinary street
was beautiful at morning, and at night
it was better.
I was not blind, I had lied.
You arrived in time, and my lies,
a circle of fishes
swam away frightened.
I wore your coat, it fit me well.
I stood taller than before
as if I had taken your proud shoulders.
With my hands in the pockets of your coat
I walked away, possessing your secrets.
Then snow began to fall, it fell
through months and long nights.

All winter I deceived you
and conspired with snow.
When I came back, with bouquets
of stiff tulips, with kisses so nervous
they burned in my mouth like broken mints,
you were gone. Your address was false.
The key would not fit into the door, the key
was a trick.
I walk under the surface of the city.
The wheels of fish return, color of ice.
Not one was lost,
because you loved me once, and now
who knows where you are,
or what was the truth?

Spider Lesson

I walked into it
when loneliness was scientific.
Figure it was love, or a spider's web.
To study its embrace
you must break the hold apart.

It is braille for sex intruders,
notebook of air,
lace cuff for the nervous wrist
that writes, "good-bye, keep out."

We whispered,
a virgin and the witch conspiring.
I flattered her, admiring
many frail, ascending wedding rings
beneath her claws.
Perhaps, I should be bride
to endlessness and admit to nothing.

Eight legs for stillness
must be thoughtless instinct.
A vain autograph refreshed
by beads of rain.
I envy her tapered waist, its ruby x,
the one initial of his name.

Underground

There is no guardrail,
often people fall.
Upon your head you can wear a light
like a miner or a mushroom picker.
You might find something
so deep and want to keep it.
Some rooms are thin as shell
gnawed by echoes. In love you leave
your voice behind. When it comes back
shivering, like special effects,
you never trust the sound of it.
Many have come before, using lies
as pickaxes,
promises leaked from stone
like pink gas, making the head ache.
Don't look for gold; anything looks bright
when you alone first find it.
Farther on, in daylight, nothing remains
important. Like this:
A man on the subway rides to work,
across the aisle a woman
going the same way. She has a funny look,
and on her hand a diamond big as a rat's eye.
The man will take one thing back
to illuminate the normal business of a day,
the curve of her mouth, or coal
on her eyelid. Beneath cities, it happens.
People are fooled by artificial night.
The lucky find a little crack
and climb out,
before the train goes down
following its arc of light.

Scarecrow

I wait for you, it's been days.
The wind has changed, I feel it
right through me. It makes quick decisions
like someone invited away.
My arms have become straw, my blood
has woven its stiff rope.
The clock in the heart
is knotting tiny fibers,
every second ties a thread to you.
Night covers me with dark cloth.
I can no longer see the comet
with its tail of bright oats.

I never planned, or expected
the worst. We stood still;
lightning pretended to ignore us,
but I was made to watch you. Rain
opened my eyes. You disappeared
like the blackbird. I see you everywhere
and nowhere.
I don't believe you were frightened.
Fear is nothing, really,
but dark wings. A shadow that cruises
the platinum wheat,
as if above a mirror it searches
for itself.

I open my arms
to your absence
and it takes me piece by piece
into its mouth.
Is this a way

long distances are fed?
As if nothing happened,
the wind, made of nothing,
chooses to hold on.

Passion Sense

DRIVING

Route 80 has mile markers. She used to drive her child just to get away. The road would be violet, a heavy sun going down, something squashed or shattered. Then colorless. Soon it would fall away, or perhaps she was the falling thing. She did it on purpose. She would count the mile markers. At first they were like baby teeth, but they stuck out sharp, reflected in the headlights. She switched to other landmarks. Sometimes the barns seemed to drift closer and then farther back from the edge of the highway, ferocious then motherly. She would count the miles between the stables, pig huts, the feed lots with white faces. A homely luminescence, and a smell that reached out in a frightened way. She understood distance. Her car had an odometer that she could reset again and again. Still traveling, she would punch it. Watch the zeros roll up. Distance was easily manipulated. There was land before her windshield, land in her rearview mirror. There was the shadow of land on her child's face. She began to understand speed. That it had nothing to do with distance, nothing to do with direction or a particular moment or location. In the car, her child slept backwards faster and faster.

ICE

In her mind there was a field of ice, it was spreading. She tried to melt it back with his presence, his body, with an idea of him. Perhaps it was something optical, after driving over a thousand acres of snow from west to east, and turning back. The wheels hot inside, yet building up with snow, a hard, pounded white. One cannot exaggerate a feeling of cold. People who almost freeze to death are not likely to embellish their stories. Not like the earthquake victim who explained how his bones shook like rubber wands, or the airline passenger who claimed that fear was like falling forward through a black arc of memory. To become cold is to become silent, your voice so small and clear it is missing. There was a young mother stranded on a mountain. She ate the snow from her palms so she could nurse her baby. The snow was like a poison, she died with a hand over her mouth. The baby lived but could tell nothing. It was the only survivor, it survived without talking.

DRIVING

When she drove the car for him he yelled at her. She was a good driver but he ridiculed her constantly. She sat stiff at the wheel and drove well. But he insisted on directing her movements and he threatened her when she did not respond accordingly. She knew it would be safer to drive for herself, faster and faster. The way she drove with her daughter, with respect for the fields and the small black shoulder of the road. If she looked in the rearview mirror he scolded her, told her to look where she was going. If she looked in front, he screamed at her for not knowing what followed them so closely. She began to let go of him. She released him little by little at each stoplight. Until she felt nothing but his shadow still tense and angry beside her. She liked to imagine something crazy. She imagined driving in South America, into the jungle. A neon penumbra simmering, his body evaporating into a hot orange light. She looked in the rearview mirror and saw the snowline melting behind her. She looked out the windshield and saw the little monkeys in sweaty vegetation, the big red orchids. Behind her she could see the cattle, taut in their fat, white-eyed. Loaded on the tractor trailers that hissed up and down with a cold, reptilian hunger. Before her there was the shimmer of a peaceable kingdom, the jungle heat like a beautiful visible flesh. But the best sight was that last view of her daughter, huddled with leopards and growing no further.

Tuesday

This is night
like a promise folded twice
in a white envelope.
Secretaries enter the dim light
of automobiles
when work is over, dark falls
into their laps
like new purchases.
Now stars appear
in small, appropriate positions.

Today a briefcase fell from its handle;
possession spilled
all illegible signatures.
I have lost the little ring
with grief's initial,
and I will drop from the hands
of my name. It was Tuesday,
virtuous third square, and December.
Thirty-one acres of snow and black
fences. Days follow days,
cornered in a white field
and forced from subway platforms.
An ice pick might open
a love letter, or a kiss
fall harmfully upon someone.
Desire has no chronologic form,
a first event reverses the outcome.
It was Tuesday, distinguished from Wednesday
by its night. Sort it by shade: asphalt,
color of slow motion, black and refusal
of black. The decision is night.

In the office, graph paper waits
for its scarlet zero.
The empty are satisfied by more
emptiness, and the sleepless wake
sleepless to telephone one another.
Yes, I have dreamed all dreams.
I sang like steam,
wasteful songs. I will go back
to work, as the hysterical maintain
blank faces long after emergencies,
as the drowned breathe evenly
with the sea.
A life seems frank, organized seven ways.
Loss keeps white, like the moon
and its memo of shame
with sentiment's frail watermark.
I won't imagine you
or in any sequence
think of us, of our days
thanked by nights.

Washed

I want to own you
but you are gone.
Say this
a hundred times.

I go to the hypnotist
refusing Buddhism.
He sold me a word,
a fifty-dollar one.
When I learn it
I will have forgotten
you.

He gives me a chunk
of tar,
he says,
"Hold this in your hand,
the one he always took,
the one he let go of."
My right hand becomes moist
and black.
He says, "This is his memory."

After each session
he takes the chunk of tar
and shuts it in a drawer.
The next time he gives it back,
it's smaller.
He says,
"See, it's working, you're learning
your word well."

But the word changes
when I repeat it
quickly,
it changes into many things.
Suddenly it's wrong,
like a collar too small for me.
It says
Skull of Milk
Bladder of Gold
Penis of Cold Ebony.
It says an entire love letter
beside a dead body.

Diving Alone

Every night she ropes the ship
to her legs.
In the lead hull of memory
blind creatures find a home.

Why do they say "drift to sleep"?
Truth could be salt,
it stings her mouth
and dissolves while she is speaking.
Faith is the raft she builds
that without her, glides away.

At night she makes preparations.
Heavy clothing is removed,
the heart becomes strict with the lungs.
Holding a deep breath keeps his ghost
like a hard body inside, helps sink her.

She learned to swim early
on the flat palms of her father.
Pelvis and breastbone, wet fingertips.
She learned to swallow without thirst,
breathe without foundation.

Why do they say "deep sleep"?
Night is a still surface
and she is beneath it.

If life is a voyage, she'll go back
and forth for violets.

If love is an anchor, she will use
his slender knife and set herself free.
If death is black water
she will see through it.

Three

Reckless Wedding

The house is white
as a sheet
under a bright stain.
Especially at night
when stars bleed
from mysterious heels
then wander off.

You married me
when outside
the forsythia slit
a thousand little wrists.
The deep tulip blew up
a whole sidewalk.
Now I look into a mirror
and see the red burning
of a skull understanding
one thing at a time.

It's true,
I watch the lawn
fill up with yellow
whips, the willow trees
that twist
and then let go.
From underground
their roots tunnel
upward,
they want to live a life backwards.

Years of This

It's like beginning small, the business
is marriage. First they buy the sign
and stack the shelves.
Her legs are long and cool
as fluorescent lights.
She sits aglow at the cash register
or with the adding machine in her lap.

People will buy anything sold in pairs.

Years of this and they buy real estate.
He builds the house and adds on and adds
on. On the patio, the children wiggle
their toes in wet cement, practicing
the names they will die with.

She is still adding and subtracting,
the lines in her palms do not lengthen
or multiply. The wrinkle in her womb
becomes the final namesake.

They started with nickels, dimes, animal
hungers. First he mowed the lawn,
she weeded. Then the gardener came
three times a week.
Now from their condominium window
a final geranium can be seen above traffic.
Its bloom tight pink
like an infant's fist behind glass.
They imagine their children returning, repentant.
All of them religious and sad.

Expedition to Sincerity

You think I plan everything,
nothing spontaneous ever nabs me.
But it's overcompensation on my part;
I grew between step-brothers, breeding
incest subtle as violets.
The single bed loses
its hospital corners.
If I organize things, it's just to keep
covered.

Even pioneers had their blueprints,
they planned to love something.
Without wood, they used mud
and packed disappointment into black
sheltering. Soon a wild grass grew
above them. I'm not so smart,
I follow the footprints and learn
ballroom dancing. In love I break
the glasses, I burn holes
in the velvet tuxedo of sex.

I was bribed
by their flashlights, and guilty,
I prayed or just played dead.
All night, a nickel twirled
upon the tight sheet, as I memorized
the same passage from my book:
A pioneer mother is trampled by horses.
On her grave they place a spokeless
wagon wheel. From there, the child
goes on without her.

Missing from Home

I'm the one they call "littlest,"
when families review losses
by accidental death or illness.

"Fat one," they named you
when the uncles came to play
pinochle with our beautiful mother.

The night before you ran away,
we went into an abandoned house
with all its lights on.
A wife had been taken by police
but her husband escaped on the B&O.

Neighbors collected
china and flatware,
and ripped the curtains loose.
You said it was stealing,
the way women smile
without showing their teeth.

I unpinned the doilies
from the chairs, knowing someone
would want them.
You kept still
before a gilt mirror,

"This makes me thin,"
you said, moving your hands
in the shape of an hourglass.

Even the principal from the school
had come to loot,
he wore his terrible blazer.
When he removed the mirror
from the wall, you became full
of something
for a moment, but it diminished.

Our mother, examining the lace,
began to laugh
and covered her face.
She said it's crazy
about sad people.

The next day,
taking no belongings,
you got into some man's
flashy car.

Faithful Excommunicates

The mothers were harder to find
they changed themselves into grape arbors, vistas,

and water holes, but I searched for the heart
and shot them there! — *Frank O'Hara*

My mother advised me, tightening
my ribbons, not to walk behind horses,
not to suck my milk money, not to wander
on the rifle range, my brothers were loading up.
And my father, mowing the lawn into wet piles,
one for each daughter, yelled —
Look out for your feet!
I collected shotgun shells
for a huge allowance, disliked dolls
with flirty eyes. But I bought them
for the fence posts, pinning them in a row.
I waited for my favorite sharpshooters.
It thrilled me, at noon an empty sun dial
and gunpowder lifting.

Grown up, my brothers are killing
their rabbits behind my eyelids,
my father pulling fists of chickweed
from my blood. I still love them.
But I pledge my heart to a man,
strange to everyone. He strings a bow.
Under the heel of his hand, it's something
forced into a smile.
I'm hungry for the apple on my head.
In love I wind into myself, thin as a target
in the distance. Thin as a pale dress

or a shadow on a Pocono mountain.
They take aim, it's always perfect and merciful.
It might split into my memory like a marriage,
or open the apple like a porcelain face.

On Sundays I take the path between God
and my mother's skin. My brothers
tape their triggers, and my sweetheart
threads his arrow. There is desire,
unnatural silence. You feel it in church,
moist in the palm of my mother's white glove.
At an altar she is snapping off her prayers
like BBs. I pledge my heart to you, my sportsmen,
angelic and stiff. My mother's silhouette darkens,
her warnings dissolve like incense and rifle smoke.
These cold red circles become my own.

The Silverside Girl

It isn't that her life was small
in any way. Twelve years is time
enough for some, although the school
was shocked and took a collection.
We stood in gym class as if in church.
To give embarrassed elegies,
we wore our ironed smocks.

My turn, I crushed the paper daffodil,
I did not hesitate.
For I knew every detail,
unashamed, her death was memorized.

It wasn't the dark cinnamon at her temple,
or the brother who yodeled so loud
for the parents.
It wasn't the lilacs that bloomed
for one week and then leached pale,
into ivory, into bone-white fists.
The evidence was simpler than this:
A black howl that frightened
the six white ponies from one end
of the field.

She was lighthearted; the pavement glittered
almost hypnotic beneath.
O seductive velocity, that moment she let go
and seemed to fly above the street.
Seven stiff blue cards clipped to the spokes,
praised her vivid as applause.
And the terrible clothespin, splintered,

which ruined the rubber wheel —
this is what we love to blame.
Well, I prefer to think of them:
six white ponies,
their muzzles turning black with summer.

No Rain in Delaware

Lawns burn, croquet hoops ignite
like small circus acts.
October turns mute, and silence spreads
through families like foam on underbrush.
The Brandywine River, parched, moves by
on its mud tongue
like a long word
someone is secretly speaking.

A girl at a carnival believes
she is traveling. In the coil of pink
tickets she keeps her wedding-ring finger
clean. The ferris wheel revolves
almost historical in red clay dust.

Count one circle each time
her hips slam the bar.
The girl is beginning to notice
herself, while candy apples gleam
at the waist of a black vendor.
At night the wheel lights up
and the girl, isolate and dark,
is winning.

Her viewpoint is steady,
although an intimate chamber
is twirling nonsensical at midnight.
Below her, exotic animals turn
in their cages, portable, mystical.
Nostrils caked with dirt detect nothing.
Fire has no smell of its own; some say
it is the secret scent of pleasure.

Smoke is moist, the subconscious breath
of peril.

Across town,
in a pretty neighborhood,
her father's yard is flaming
toward her room.
The heat just under control
runs orange and black around the house,
wild and seductive as the tiger.

Reunion

How happy we were, and happier still
to have a photograph,
for it was proof: *That's us,*
that's the place. The place we met!
A moment surrounded by nothing
but white, a promise
contained and bordered,
how we loved to hold it
to the light.
A crisp, authoritative scent
of something new, like the odor
in medical rooms
where small, painless operations
take place.
But, it's different to find a drawer
unlocked, and in it a picture album,
the family all together as before.
It might be an attic, or some room
too small to share.
You find it alone, and examine
whole summers recklessly fastened
to one page,
winters assembled and put aside
in white envelopes.
Some seem to squint
at every celebration.
How cruel the way in which the children
are lined up
in rows by height, the way aunts press
their pets hard against their waists.
A mother's face is beautiful
but now that certain facts are known,

her smile looks mostly discipline.
Singled out, and seated on a swing,
a girl glides backwards through still air,
through everyone
and farther, many years.
Gathered like wreaths upon steep lawns,
they seem aware of death
and hold their breath.

Elegy for Mothers and Orphans

My memory is quick as breath
on cold water,
but yours is relaxed
as if all things you know
have organized like scum
at the lip of a waterfall.

You can't remember
a mother's grim lace,
or being sliced out
with the hot rim of sodium pentothal.
Your mother grew as she undressed
button by button, until your birth.
Then she put on her heavy coat for forty years.

Beach cottage shingle, sugared
with a plaque of sand. Blue jaw
of Cape Cod bay, holding clean
five children lined up
like breakwater into the sea.

And if you didn't love me, don't begin.

Starfish and pebbles slip
through linings. Starfish
with one bright eye in its neck
and pointing in five directions.
Your life, a collection on a bureau glass
reflecting God
or his tiny fossil.

I'll tell you what I know
but nothing
that might wake you.
As you drift beyond us
like music of the sea
through old arguments,
five figures rise to the surface.
Only their shadows
do not leave them.